The Rarie

A story adapted from an old Irish pun

Story by Arthur Lee Quinn
Illustrations by Colby Green

Surrogate Press®

Story © 2020 Arthur Lee Quinn
Illustrations © 2020 Colby Green
All rights reserved.

No part of this publication may be reproduced, stored in a retrieval system,
or transmitted in any form or by any means, electronic, mechanical,
photocopying, recording, or otherwise,
without written permission of the author and illustrator.
www.SurrogatePress.com

Published in the United States by
Surrogate Press®
an imprint of Faceted Press®
Surrogate Press, LLC
Park City, Utah
www.SurrogatePress.com

Library of Congress Control Number: 2019917117

The Rarie / Story by Arthur Lee Quinn / Illustrated by Colby Green

ISBN: 978-1-947459-31-1

Printed in the United States of America
by Kindle Direct Publishing

Book design by Katie Mullaly, Surrogate Press®

To Sharon
My Wild Irish Rose

Some time, but not too long ago, on a lovely little farm in southern Ireland, lived Mr. and Mrs. O'Malley and their two children, Brendan and Bridget. The farm, which had been in the family for over a hundred years, had beautiful green rolling hills that went down to banks of the River Suir. The farmhouse sat in the center of the quilted fields and was sturdy and cozy.

Brendan and Bridget led quiet, happy lives. Besides doing their daily farm chores, they went to school and played with their friends. And their pets – a dog named Seamus and Fiona the cat – kept them company.

In the evenings, after the children had gone to bed, Mr. and Mrs. O'Malley would sit by the fire – Mrs. O'Malley knitting and Mr. O'Malley reading. Since this was before television, the couple would also listen to the radio and to their precious collection of phonograph records. They had recordings of all of the popular tunes from over the years.

These recorded songs were their greatest source of pleasure. Mr. O'Malley favored lively war tunes, and Mrs. O'Malley preferred Irish ballads.

The family loved the river that bordered their farm almost as much as they loved their songs. So sometimes, when the weather was good, they would turn the phonograph up high, open the doors and windows, and stroll down to the riverbank, listening to the music the whole way.

Early one foggy summer morning, Bridget thought she heard a noise at the back door. She opened it and looked down at the stoop to find a basket covered by a blanket. Pulling the blanket aside, Bridget found a ball of grey fur with a note. It read simply, "Please take care of our rarie."

Bridget took the basket inside and showed it to Brendan, who asked, "What in the world is a rarie?" The creature was warm and cuddly and seemed to be alive, although it had no head, arms, or legs. It was just a round ball of fur. The children showed it to their parents, placed it by the fire, and watched it for a time. But it remained completely still.

Seamus and Fiona sniffed curiously at the new arrival, but did not seem bothered by it. At first, Fiona thought it a toy and lifted it out of the basket and rolled it around on the floor, much as she would a ball of yarn. Bridget scolded Fiona and told her to leave the new pet – whatever it was – alone.

The O'Malleys showed the creature to their neighbors and relatives and asked if they had ever heard of a "rarie." None had, and several said they ought to get rid of the thing. But it so fascinated the children that they were allowed to keep it.

Neither the children nor the parents knew how to care for the rarie, other than to keep it warm and comfortable. But one evening – just to see if anything would happen – they put a bowl of milk beside the basket.

No one saw the rarie move, but – sure enough – the next morning, the milk bowl was empty. So the children repeated this ritual every night, and the rarie appeared to grow a little each day.

In time, the family and the pets became used to their silent friend. The children loved to stroke its warm fur; Seamus and Fiona generally ignored it, other than to occasionally sniff or lick it. Everyone came to accept it as one of them.

One day, Uncle Finbar from Dublin stopped by to visit. The children ran to meet him at the door, excitedly telling him about the rarie and how it was slowly but steadily growing. When he saw it by the fire, his face became pale, and he sunk into a chair, growling, "Get rid of it now. It's dangerous!"

It seems that many years before, while in a pub, Uncle Finbar had overheard a dark and very sinister stranger tell a scary tale about a creature like the rarie. A kind old couple, finding a live ball of fur, had taken it in, cared for it, and fed it. Like the O'Malley's rarie, this creature never seemed to move, but grew steadily bigger over time. But when it became so big that they could hardly lift it, they became frightened.

So, with the help of friends, the old couple put the creature into the bed of a truck and pushed the entire vehicle over a cliff into the ocean. They swore it screamed on the way down. Uncle Finbar admitted that at the time he dismissed the story as a tall tale. But now – seeing one – he forebodingly said, "Don't take any chances; dump the thing into the river."

Despite Uncle Finbar's somber warning, the O'Malleys could not bring themselves to destroy the rarie. In fact, they only became more attached to – and protective of – the creature.

Summer became fall, and the creature continued to grow. Brendan and Bridget wondered what would happen if they started giving the rarie food in addition to the milk, so one evening, they set out a plate of cookies.

Lo and behold, the next morning, the plate was clean. The children knew Seamus and Fiona had not eaten the cookies because the pets had slept in their bedroom. The rarie had eaten the food! Now what? The children continued to put food out each night, always finding it gone the next morning. And the rarie continued to grow.

As time went on, the O'Malleys did not much discuss the ever-swelling fur ball that shared their home. But in the evenings, as they tried to relax and enjoy their records, Mr. and Mrs. O'Malley would eye it nervously. What if the story Uncle Finbar had overheard was true? Relatives and friends also expressed concern. So they decided to telephone their uncle again to ask his advice. Upon his return to the home, Uncle Finbar was shocked to see how much the critter had grown.

Brendan and Bridget, who were as attached to the fur ball as their parents were wary, argued with Uncle Finbar about its fate. He insisted "it" must "be disposed of," but they insisted on keeping it. It hadn't harmed anyone, they protested! It was peaceful, quiet, clean, and absolutely no trouble. The children held firm, and, after two days of trying to convince them otherwise, Uncle Finbar gave up and went home.

A few nights later, the children heard Seamus growl. He was snarling at the rarie, something he had never done before. Bridget poked the creature with her finger and actually thought she saw it move just the slightest bit. But nothing else happened. Then Mr. O'Malley poked it. Still no movement. After the family had stared at the ball of fur for a long while, they left the milk and food, as was customary, and went to bed.

The next day, the O'Malleys could hardly keep their eyes off the rarie, so curious were they to see if it would move or make any sounds. And this time, they did see it move, if only slightly. But it wasn't just that, they all heard it make a growling sound. What was happening to the creature?

That night, they left a bowl of milk by the basket, but no food. As fascinated as they were, Mr. and Mrs. O'Malley were also very concerned. No, they were scared. The couple debated long into the night about what to do. Bleary-eyed and exhausted, they finally decided to sleep on it and leave the decision to the morning.

In the morning, Mr. and Mrs. O'Malley again talked the matter over and finally reached a decision. The parents decided they just couldn't risk what may come. The rarie had to go.

But what about the children, and how and when to do it? They decided Uncle Finbar's idea was a good (if cruel) one. They would push the rarie into the river. To avoid the children's protestations and tears — of which there would surely be many — Mr. and Mrs. O'Malley determined to sneak out that night to complete the deed, and would wait until the next morning to tell Brendan and Bridget.

Mr. and Mrs. O'Malley were sick with worry all the day long. They were kind, generous people, and the thought of destroying a living thing — and breaking their two children's hearts in the process — was almost too much to bear. But what else could they do? Every soul they consulted, save their own children, agreed with Uncle Finbar. Pushing the creature into the river was the only answer.

When they knew their children to be sound asleep, the O'Malleys began their grim task. But only then did they realize how difficult it would be: the rarie had grown so big, it had become rather unwieldy. Together, they rolled the rarie from its place by the fire to the cottage entrance. It barely fit through the doorway, it had grown so enormous.

Once outside, the O'Malleys rolled the rarie onto the path leading to the river. But the path went uphill, making the task all the more difficult. And how much longer it seemed in the moonlight than it did during the day! The couple huffed and puffed and pushed the rarie along. Finally they neared the bluff above the water.

The couple paused to catch their breath, and Mrs. O'Malley said simply, "I didn't realize it was such a long way." They looked at each other, both dreading what they had to do next. Finally Mr. O'Malley gathered his resolve and said, "Are we ready to tip it over?" But at those words, the rarie suddenly moved! The couple froze in fear, then both fell backward from the shock. The creature rose slowly from the ground on two short, hairy legs that unfolded from the bottom of its fur body.

Two arms popped out from its sides, and a pair of huge round eyes suddenly appeared at the top of the hairy bod. A moment later, a gaping mouth opened in the monster's middle – and it smiled the biggest smile they had ever seen.

The beast slowly approached the terrified
couple, stopping just in front of them. Then it
began to sing:

"It's a long way to Tipperary,
It's a long way to go.
It's a long way to Tipperary,
To the sweetest girl I know!
Goodbye, Piccadilly,
Farewell, Leicester Square!
It's a long, long way to Tipperary,
But my heart's right there!"

The rarie was singing Mr. O'Malley's favorite song! The family lived in County Tipperary! The creature knew all of the verses, and — amazingly — sang with the same voice as on the record.

Once it finished, the rarie bowed to them. After a painful silence, the shocked but delighted pair asked timidly, "Do you know any more songs?"

The rarie accommodated them gladly, bursting forth with "The Rose of Tralee," Mrs. O'Malley's favorite. Once again it sang in perfect imitation of the voice on the record. The rarie sang and sang and then sang some more. It seemed to know every song from the O'Malley's record collection.

Mr. and Mrs. O'Malley joined hands with the rarie, and the trio sang all the way back to the house. The noise woke the children, who rushed outside. They couldn't believe their eyes. The rarie had come alive and was singing! Little did they know their parents had come so close to making a terrible mistake.

The rarie became a beloved part of the family. It stopped growing and was content to roll up in a ball and rest by the fire until asked to perform. The O'Malleys never did see it eat or drink, but whatever they left out at night was always gone in the morning.

The rarie's reputation spread far and wide across the country, and the O'Malleys graciously greeted the many visitors who traveled to their home to hear it perform. Even Uncle Finbar came down from Dublin, and he always delighted when he heard it sing "It's a Long Way to Tipperary."

The End

About the Author

Arthur Lee Quinn practiced law in Washington, D.C., for more than forty years, then spent ten years as an international business consultant. In both capacities, he specialized in representing agricultural interests in emerging economies, an exciting and rewarding career that took him to countries across the Americas, as well as Afghanistan and the American West and Midwest. Arthur derived great satisfaction from this work and took special pride in helping establish community-centered agriculture programs.

Throughout his professional career, Arthur also nurtured a desire to work with stories, especially those drawn from his own life experiences. His early efforts included a series of screenplay treatments that dramatized some of the more memorable cases from his time as a U.S. Air Force Judge Advocate at the end of the Korean War.

As someone who has always appreciated the inherent wisdom of youth, Arthur also discovered a love for writing children's stories. To-date, he has written five picture books and one chapter book for young readers—all of which were inspired by, written for, or dedicated to his six children and five grandchildren. The Rarie is the first to be illustrated and published.

Arthur has a B.S. in economics from Villanova University and a J.D. from Georgetown University Law School. He currently resides in Park City, Utah.

About the Illustrator

Fueled by caffeine and anxiety and new to the industry, Colby Green creates snail and non-snail related illustrations for Surrogate Press®.

Colby sees art as a way to convey an idea and thought that teach a lesson. He uses his art to inspire people to read and learn, especially women, minorities, and other groups that may not have all the opportunities that they should. He believes that anyone can be inspired to be their best self through the gifts that books give us.

As far as his own inspirations go, he has been influenced by other writers and artists who have worked in children's books. Writers such as Lemony Snicket and Roald Dahl. Artists such as Quentin Blake and Land of ...Children's Books® very own Toby Allen. There are many creators who contribute to the greater education of the children of the world and Colby wants to be a part of that.

"About 12 years ago I started drawing after seeing fanart on a game website. It started as a hobby more than anything, but seeing the children's books created at the time, I found myself being inspired, and more so when my nieces and nephews were born. I wanted to instill in them the love of learning that inspired me to learn when I was young."

Colby has a Bachelor's of Science in Psychology from Brigham Young University-Idaho, located in Rexburg, Idaho. He hopes to soon start work on his Masters and a PhD degree in psychology, although art is his main passion. He spends as much time as he can each day learning artistic techniques and creating art.

Contact Colby at *ColbyGreen1984@gmail.com* or feel free to message him on Twitter and Instagram at snailbunnydesigns.

Made in the USA
Columbia, SC
13 August 2021

43039151R10038